Where's the Elephant?

BARROUX

Where's the Elephant?

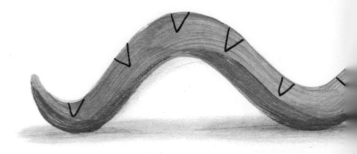

WHERE'S the PARROT?

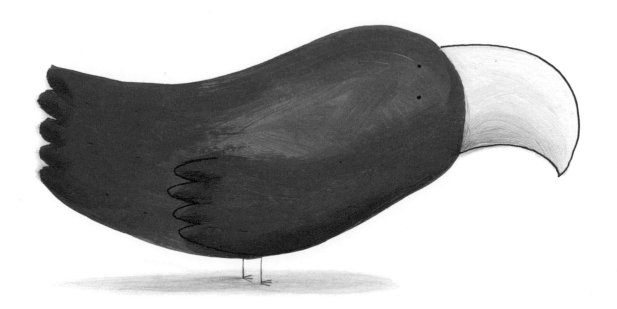

WHERE'S the SNAKE?

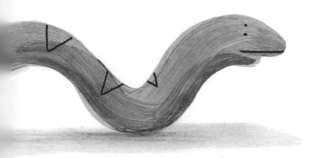

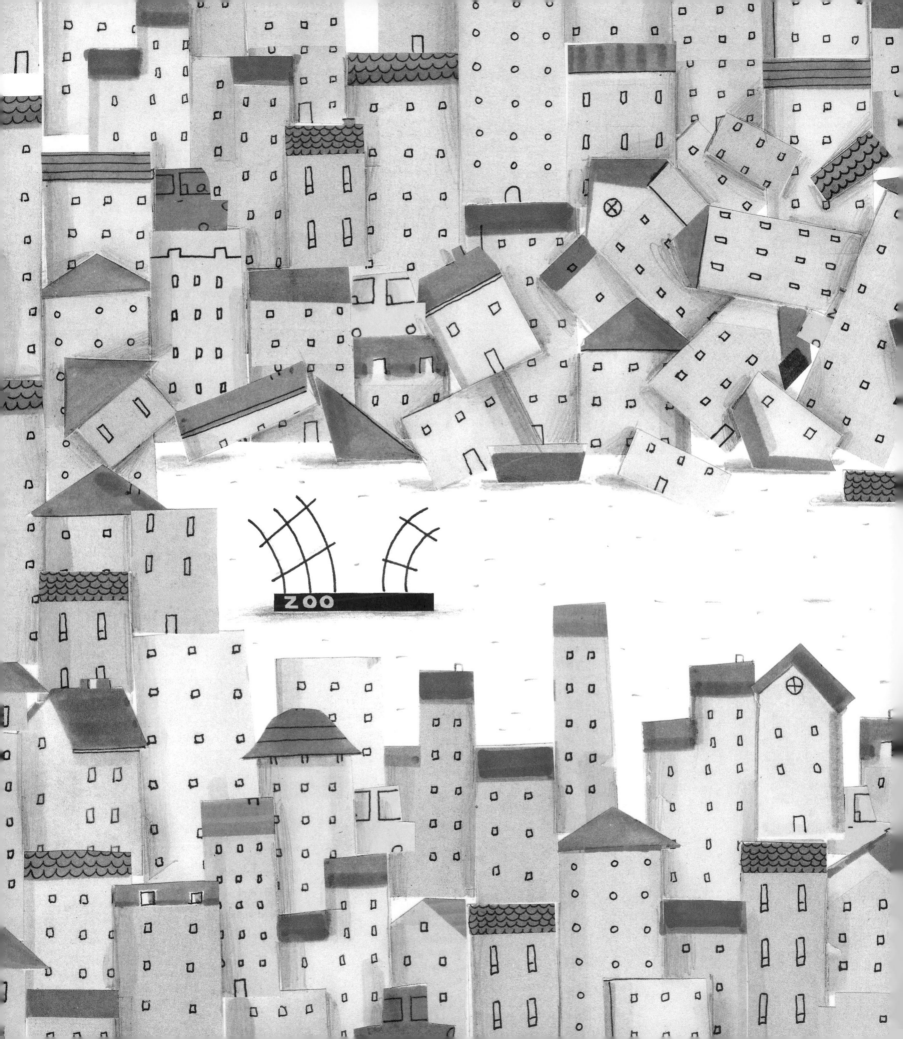
ZOO

THE STORY BEHIND THIS BOOK

When I visited Brazil five years ago, I saw parts of the Amazon rain forest set on fire to clear the way for soybean production.

Since then I have searched for a way to talk about deforestation, but it wasn't until two years ago, at the Edinburgh Book Festival, that I found my inspiration. Suddenly everything was clear in my mind and I started the first sketches . . .

Barroux

To Marguerite, Annabelle, and Milan

Copyright © 2015 by Stéphane-Yves Barroux

All rights reserved. No part of this book may be reproduced, transmitted, or stored in an information retrieval system in any form or by any means, graphic, electronic, or mechanical, including photocopying, taping, and recording, without prior written permission from the publisher.

First U.S. edition 2016
First published in Great Britain in 2015 by Egmont Books Ltd.

Library of Congress Catalog Card Number 2015937233
ISBN 978-0-7636-8110-4

TWP 20 19 18 17 16 15
10 9 8 7 6 5 4 3 2 1

Printed in Johor Bahru, Malaysia

This book was typeset in Corndog Clean.
The illustrations were done in collage, acrylic, and pencil.

Candlewick Press
99 Dover Street
Somerville, Massachusetts 02144

visit us at www.candlewick.com

CANDLEWICK PRESS